Happy Birth
Jesse Bear!

Happy Birthday, Jesse Bear!

by Nancy White Carlstrom
illustrated by Bruce Degen

ALADDIN PAPERBACKS

New York London Toronto Sydney Singapore

Other Jesse Bear books by Nancy White Carlstrom,
illustrated by Bruce Degen

Jesse Bear, What Will You Wear?
Better Not Get Wet, Jesse Bear
It's About Time, Jesse Bear
How Do You Say It Today, Jesse Bear?
Let's Count It Out, Jesse Bear

First Aladdin Paperbacks edition March 2000

Text copyright © 1994 by Nancy White Carlstrom
Illustrations copyright © 1994 by Bruce Degen

Aladdin Paperbacks
An imprint of Simon & Schuster
Children's Publishing Division
1230 Avenue of the Americas
New York, NY 10020

The Library of Congress has cataloged the hardcover edition as follows:
Carlstrom, Nancy White
Happy birthday, Jesse Bear! / by Nancy White Carlstrom ; illustrated by Bruce Degen.—1st ed.
Summary: Rhyming text and illustrations describe all the activities
associated with Jesse Bear's birthday party.
ISBN 0-02-717277-5 (hc.)
[1. Bears—Fiction. 2. Birthdays—Fiction.
3. Parties—Fiction. 4. Stories in rhyme.]
I. Degen, Bruce, ill.   II. Title.
PZ8.3.C194Hap   1994   [E]—dc20   93-25180
ISBN 0-689-83311-3 (Aladdin pbk.)

There's going to be a party,
Hope that you can come.
Games and party favors,
Birthday cake and fun.

Letters in the mailbox,
Prizes from the store,

House is decorated,
Banner on the door.

Cake is in the oven,
Air is in balloons,

Jesse's tired of waiting,
Guests should be here soon.

Time for the party,
Hope they won't be late.
Hurry up and come,
'Cause Jesse hates to wait!

One friend brings a package—
Paper wrapped and tied.
Another brings a box
With a smaller box inside.

One brings a tube,
And one brings a bag.
One brings a kite
With a birthday tag.

Tear off the paper,
Tear off the string,

Open up the boxes,
Play with everything.

Build up the blocks
As the kite flutters down.

Zoom flies the plane,
While the truck rolls to town.

Jesse's turn to give gifts,
Each with a name.
Put them on the table
And get ready for the games.

Treasure hunt with pictures,
Follow all the clues.

Open up the basket,
Hats and poppers, too.

Mama lights the candles,
Jesse makes a wish,

Papa clicks a picture,
Cake on every dish.

Happy, Happy Birthday,
From Mama, Papa, too.

Happy Birthday, Jesse Bear,
A book that's just for you!

Here's three cheers for birthdays,
Parties should not end.
Happy Birthday, Jesse Bear,
Happy Birthday, friend!